JD10 16

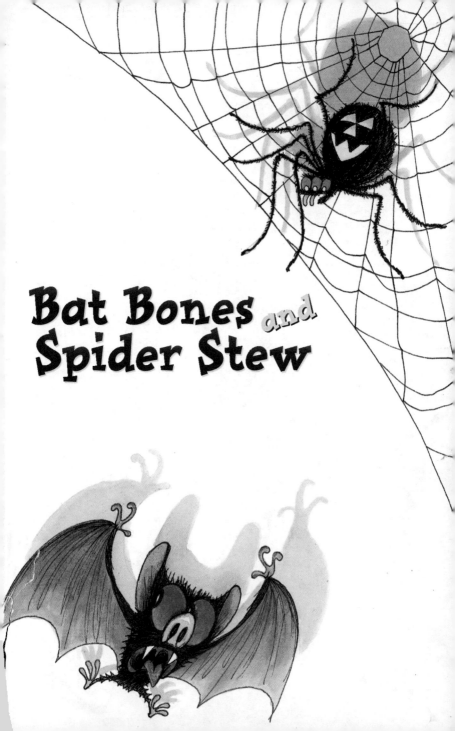

Bat Bones and Spider Stew

Michelle Poploff

Bat Bones and Spider Stew

illustrated by Bill Basso

A Yearling First Choice Chapter Book

To Karen, Jeanette, Fiona,
Barbara, and Patrice—
fangs for everything.
　　　　　—M.J. P.

To my mom, sweet Adaline,
Born in October, nineteen o nine
A little before Halloween time.
　　　　　—B.B.

Published by
Bantam Doubleday Dell Publishing Group, Inc.
1540 Broadway
New York, New York 10036
Text copyright © 1998 by Michelle Poploff
Illustrations copyright © 1998 by Bill Basso
All rights reserved.

Library of Congress Cataloging-in-Publication Data
Cataloging-in-Publication Data is available from the U.S. Library of Congress
ISBN 0-385-32557-6 (hardcover); ISBN 0-440-41440-7 (paperback)

Hardcover: The trademark Delacorte Press® is registered in the U.S. Patent
and Trademark Office and in other countries.
Paperback: The trademark Yearling® is registered in the U.S. Patent and
Trademark Office and in other countries.

Visit us on the Web! www.bdd.com
Educators and librarians, visit the BDD Teacher's Resource Center at
www.bdd.com/teachers

The text of this book is set in 17-point Baskerville.
Manufactured in the United States of America
October 1998
10 9 8 7 6 5 4 3 2 1

Contents

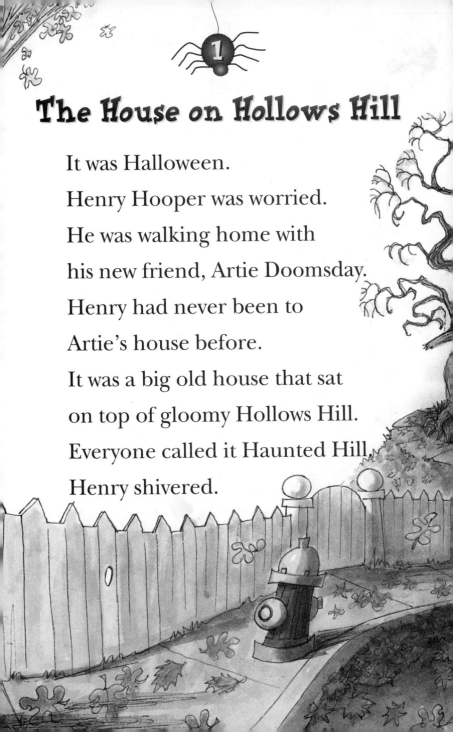

The House on Hollows Hill

It was Halloween.

Henry Hooper was worried.

He was walking home with
his new friend, Artie Doomsday.

Henry had never been to
Artie's house before.

It was a big old house that sat
on top of gloomy Hollows Hill.

Everyone called it Haunted Hill.

Henry shivered.

"Come on, slowpoke," said Artie.

"Granny can't wait to meet you."

Henry had no choice.

He walked faster.

He hoped Artie didn't hear

his teeth chattering.

If only he could think of a joke.

Henry and Artie liked monster riddles.

It didn't matter if

they were silly or scary.

"Hey," said Artie.

"What ride do ghosts like best?"

Henry thought a second.

"The roller ghoster," he said.

They slapped high fives.

Henry took a deep breath.

Once they had some riddles rolling,

maybe he'd feel better.

"Why was the baby vampire crying?"

Artie shrugged.

"He just had a bitemare," a voice said.

Henry spun around.

There was nothing there but a tree.

"Who said that?" he whispered.

"That's my sister, Wanda," said Artie.

He pointed up at the tree.

Henry thought he saw a giant bat
hanging upside down.

Artie's sister jumped off the branch.

She was dressed like a vampire.

She swirled her purple cape

and stuck out her fake fangs.

Henry stepped back.

Maybe those fangs weren't fake at all.

"Hi, Henry," Wanda said.
"That was a good riddle."
Wanda gave Henry a push.
"Come inside and meet Granny.
She's been waiting for you."
That's what I'm afraid of,
thought Henry.

Halloween Hic-Hic-Hiccups

Granny Doomsday opened the door.

She wore an old witch's hat

and a long dark dress.

"You must be Henry," she said.

They shook hands.

Granny's hand was cold and bony.

Henry's was cold and sweaty.

Granny laughed a witchy laugh.

Henry wanted to run.

"My, you're pale as a ghost," she said.

"Let me give you something to eat."

Henry tried to speak,

but a hiccup came out instead.

"*Hic,* excuse me," he said. *"Hic, hic."*

Granny winked at Artie and Wanda.

"I've made special spooky

Halloween treats for us to gobble."

"Wh-What? *Hic, hic,*" said Henry.

"Some munchy crunchy

monkey meat, topped off with

chopped-off chicken's feet.

Care for cream of snake eye soup?

It makes your tummy loop-the-loop."

Granny pointed at Henry.

"You must taste my spider stew."

"You *hic* cooked spiders?" he said.

Wanda rubbed her stomach.

"It's spider-ific." she said.

"That's just Granny's way of joking,"
said Artie. "Wanda's kidding too."

"Sure I am," said Wanda.
"Hey, bet you don't know
how to make a strawberry shake."
"*Hic,* how?" asked Henry.
"Take it to a scary movie," Wanda said.
"That's a *hic* good one," said Henry.

Granny tapped her witch's hat.
"How do you like my outfit?"
She laughed her cackly laugh.
"It's been in my family for years."
Henry's knees felt rubbery.
He quickly sat down.
"It's a perfect fit," said Artie.

"It's you, Granny," said Wanda.

Henry wondered if Granny Doomsday
was a real witch.

If she was, he was out of there.

Henry tried asking Artie.

But all that came out was

"Hic, hic, hic. Hic, hic."

Riddle-go-round

"Please pass the bat bones,"
said Wanda.

Henry nearly dropped the plate.

"Relax, pal," said Artie.

"Those bat bones are french fries.

On Halloween Granny gives
regular food creepy names.

You have to try everything."

Uh-oh, thought Henry.

He quietly sniffed his food.

It smelled good and looked okay.

The creepy names were just jokes.

He had to be brave.

The first bite tasted good.

"I have a *hic* riddle," he said.

"What do *hic* witches eat at the beach?"

All three Doomsdays looked at him.

"*Hic,* sand-witches," he said.

24

"Hee hee," said Granny.

"I'll have to remember that one."

She leaned over to Henry.

"Try my tutti-frutti rattail meat.

It's really a roast turkey treat."

25

Wanda took out her fangs.
"I don't know how vampires
can eat with these things," she said.
"Guess what's for dessert?"
Before Henry could answer,
she yelled, *"Booberry pie and I scream!"*

"Shush, now, Wanda," said Granny.

"How can we stop Henry's hiccups?"

"I always get *hic* hiccup attacks

when I'm *hic* nervous," said Henry.

His stomach gurgled.

He ate some more food.

"Let's have a Halloween
riddle-go-round," said Artie.
"Everyone takes a turn telling a riddle.
You're our guest, Henry. Go ahead."
Henry looked at the jack-o'-lantern.
A candle glowed inside.
"What's orange and falls off walls?"
The Doomsdays didn't know.
"*Hic,* Humpty Pumpkin," said Henry.

"I'm next," said Wanda.

"Where does a witch buy stamps?"

"At the ghost office,"

said Artie and Henry.

"No fair," said Wanda.

"My turn," said Artie.

"Why was the baby monster sad?"

When no one answered, he said,

"Because he missed his mummy."

"*Hic*, not bad," said Henry.

He smiled and tried to relax.

That's when the lights went out.

Monster Milk Shake

Somewhere a door banged.

The wind whistled. The cat meowed.

Henry jumped up and something
grabbed him.

It was Granny Doomsday's bony hand.

"Don't worry," she said.

"It's only the wind."

Granny helped Henry into his chair.

She lit some more jack-o'-lanterns.

Shadows danced on the walls.

Granny brought Henry a tall drink.

"Try my special monster milk shake.

Drink every drop," she said.

"You'll feel much better after you do."

Henry's throat felt very dry.

He took three long swallows.

"You take a turn now, Granny,"

said Wanda. Granny nodded.

"What's a ghost's favorite drink?"

"Ghoul-Aid," said Henry and Wanda.

Granny cackled. "I can't fool you."

Soon Henry felt cozy and full.

He liked trading riddles by candlelight.

"Last round," said Artie.

"Where do goblins do the
dead man's float?"

"In a swimming ghoul," said Granny.

Wanda clicked her fangs.

"What's a vampire's favorite holiday?"

"Fangs-giving day," said Henry.

"Oh, rats," said Wanda.

"What's black and white and
red all over?" Henry asked.

"A sunburned skeleton," said Artie.

"Shucks," said Henry.

"I'm last," said Granny.

"What do monsters have that
no one else has?"

"Baby monsters," said Henry.

"That's an old one."

Suddenly the lights came on again.

Everyone blinked.

Henry looked at his plate.

He had finished all the food

and drunk the last drop

of his monster milk shake.

Granny turned to Henry.

She looked into his eyes and said,

"It's all over for you now, Henry."

Henry looked at the Doomsdays.

"What's over?" he croaked.

"Hiccups!" they all shouted.

Henry jumped up from his seat.

"You're right," he said.

"I'm over the hiccups."

Henry grinned.

"Fangs for everything, Granny."

He shook her bony hand.

This time it felt warm.

Zombie Smiles

"Come on, Henry," Artie said.

"Let's get ready for trick-or-treat."

Henry and Artie put on black shirts

painted with white skeleton bones.

They wore old black jeans

painted with glowing bones.

Wanda poked her head in.

"May I come too?" she asked.

Artie looked at Henry.

"Do you mind if Wanda tags along?"

Wanda grinned and her fangs fell out.

Henry laughed. "Fine with me."

"Yahoo!" Wanda yelled.

"I'll have my costume on in a jiffy."

"Isn't *that* your costume?" asked Henry.

"You'll find out." Wanda grinned.

Soon the two skeleton boys and
Wanda, dressed as a witch, went
downstairs with their treat bags.
Granny Doomsday had a camera.
"Line up for some pictures," she said.
"Everyone smile and say, 'Zombie.'"
"*Zombie!*" they shouted.

Granny took three pictures.

"Here, Henry, you may keep this one."

Henry saw two skeleton boys.

"Where's Wanda?" he asked.

"She was right behind me."

Something wiggled down his back.

"Aagh!" Henry jumped.

Wanda popped out from behind a plant.

"What's purple and green and hairy?"

"I don't know," Henry said.

"I don't know either,

but it's crawling down your back."

Henry hopped around.

Wanda couldn't stop laughing.

Granny opened the front door.

"Do drop in at the Doomsdays' again.

Next time you'll be our dinner ghost—

I mean guest. I'll make my

lip-smacking *ghoul*-ash," said Granny.

"You Doomsdays are fun, but weird,"

said Henry. He turned to Artie.

"I'll race you down Haunted—

I mean Hollows Hill.

Let's go, Wanda Witch."

Wanda was still laughing.

"Wait *hic* up for *hic* me," she said.

"Oh *hic* no *hic*. Now I've *hic* got them."

Wanda Witch chased Henry and Artie.

She hiccuped all the way

down Hollows Hill.

Monster Milk Shake Recipe

1 cup of milk
1 cup of seltzer
1/2 cup of fruit-flavored frozen yogurt
2 tablespoons of honey
1 tablespoon of chocolate syrup

Mix well.*

*This is a delicious snack but is not
guaranteed to cure hiccups.